THELONIOUS MOUSE

THELONIOUS MOUSE

Orel Protopopescu

Pictures by Anne Wilsdorf

Farrar Straus Giroux ♪ New York

In memory of my friend Jackie Raven, poet and dancer,
who tapped her way through life
—O.P.

Text copyright © 2011 by Orel Protopopescu
Pictures copyright © 2011 by Anne Wilsdorf
All rights reserved
Distributed in Canada by D&M Publishers, Inc.
Printed in February 2011 in China by Macmillan Production (Asia) Ltd.,
Kwun Tong, Kowloon, Hong Kong (Supplier Code: 10)
Designed by Andrew Arnold
First edition, 2011
1 3 5 7 9 10 8 6 4 2

www.fsgkidsbooks.com

Library of Congress Cataloging-in-Publication Data
Protopopescu, Orel Odinov.
    Thelonious Mouse / Orel Protopopescu ; pictures by Anne Wilsdorf. — 1st ed.
        p.   cm.
    Summary: Thelonious is a hipster mouse who cannot keep himself from taunting the cat of the house,
but once Thelonious discovers a toy piano, he and the cat make some beautiful music together.
    ISBN: 978-0-374-37447-1
    [1. Mice—Fiction.   2. Cats—Fiction.   3. Music—Fiction.]   I. Wilsdorf, Anne, ill.   II. Title.

PZ7.P9438Th 2011
[E]—dc22
                                                                                            2009047599

Thelonious was some cool cat—for a mouse.

Whenever Fat Cat snored up her usual storm, Thelonious's whole family went pitter-patter across the floor.

Not Thelonious. He pounded four paws and sang,

"Scat cat! Sceee-at! Snap a trap to catch a fat-tat tatter-tailed cat!"

"Hush up, Thelonious," his mama said.

"You'll wake the cat!" his daddy warned.

But Thelonious had too much music in him to stuff into a mousehole. He had to let it out.

He tap-danced and pranced on the floor—

"Squish a bag of fishy old bratty catty rat-a-tatty!"

—while his sister and brothers collected scraps.

He clapped and slapped the walls—

"Bite a bit of bitter old hang-fanged litter-box sitter!"

He skittered and twittered on top of a tea table while Fat Cat took
her afternoon nap.

"Nibblety dribblety cheesit! Icky ticky old fleabit!"

Fat Cat opened one sleepy eye.
"Come home, Thelonious!" his parents cried before Fat Cat opened
the other eye—wide.

She jumped like someone had lit her tail!

Thelonious raced for home, but that old cat was close. He could smell her tuna breath.

Still, Thelonious *had* to slide his tail across the floor. He simply *had* to. The sound it made was so delicious.

Swish-cheese . . . Swish-cheese . . .

Fat Cat swatted at his tail with razor claws.

Back and forth, Thelonious snaked his tail. He liked the swing it gave to his sound.

Swish-a-whisker . . . Swish-a-whisker . . .

Fat Cat pounced,
too far right.

She pounced again, too far left.

Swish-a-pounce . . . Swish-a-pounce . . .

Faster and faster,
Thelonious played with her.

Swish-a-pounce-a-swish-a-pounce-a—

SPLAT!

Thelonious slapped the tip of his tail against the wall, right under Fat Cat's nose, then slid into his mousehole. That *splat!* said the song was over. That *splat!* said Thelonious was cool.

"That *splat!* will get you caught one day!" his mama squeaked.

"Next time you'll lose your tail!" his daddy fumed.

"But I won't lose the beat," Thelonious said.

And so it went, day after day. He was so smooth, always in the groove, but he was in there all by himself. "Sing and dance with me for your supper," he told his sister and brothers one evening.

"Greasy cheese and cheesy peas, cat-tripping drippings,

chocolate-chip crumbs, buttery batter, and yum-yummy buns . . ."

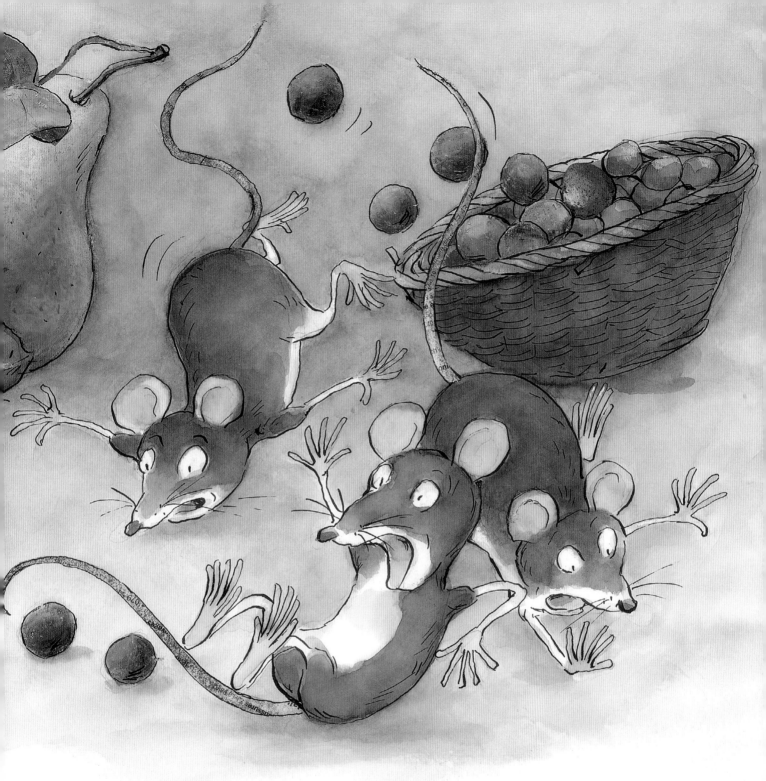

But they couldn't keep the beat. Their tongues tied, the song died, and they fell all over their feet.

"That old Fat Cat has more rhythm than you guys," Thelonious moaned.

"So play with her, you fool," they said, tittering behind their paws.

"*Nobody's fool, I'm bold!*
I am so cool, I'm cold!"
sang Thelonious, pounding the floor in a rage.

Fat Cat jumped off the window seat and landed with a thump. A soft sound, but off the beat.

Thelonious turned to see who was messing with his music. A whiff of sardine came at him with twelve pounds of furry fury that blocked his way home! Thelonious ran through the living room to the playroom.

What to do? What to do?

Fat Cat was in the air, claws screaming, teeth gleaming! Thelonious leaped through the window of a dollhouse.

Fat Cat howled. She pounded the house, shaking and raking.

Thelonious bounced on a bed, just his size. It made such a heart-stopping boppity-bop-bop! He twirled his tail like a lasso and sang,

"Cat's a flop! Too fat to stop a bouncy mousy whip-whopping nonstop bebop!"

Hours later, even Thelonious was tired. How to put that flabby old crabby tabby to sleep? Jumping a little lower, singing a little slower, he crooned a lullaby,

"Hickory, dickory, wind down the clock, tick by tick and tock by tock . . ."

Fat Cat poked her nose inside the window, breathing in rhythm with Thelonious's lagging, dragging song . . .

When Fat Cat was snoring, Thelonious climbed out the window and tiptoed home, quiet as a mouse for the first time in his life.

"Thelonious!" his parents said. "We thought you were trapped!" They sobbed and hugged him. "That cat will get you if you don't watch out!"

But Thelonious *had* to get back to that bouncy dollhouse bed. He simply *had* to.

The next day, while Fat Cat napped, Thelonious sneaked into the playroom, but the dollhouse was on top of a toy chest! Luckily, there was a box on the floor next to it. Never stumped, Thelonious jumped.

The box had black and white steps, but they didn't seem to climb anywhere. Each step rang out as he ran, hitting higher and higher notes.

He didn't hear the thump as Fat Cat woke up. He pranced and danced and sang,

"What is this ringing, singing thing that swings me crooning to the tuneful moon?"

Fat Cat stared at that bobbing bopper. With one bite she could snap him in two.

"A click-a-keys, a lick-a-cheese, a jingling, tingling sends me in a swoon,"

Thelonious crooned, until something fishy made his nose twitch.

He turned around.
Two big eyes stared back at him.

What to do? What to do? What to doobee-doobee-doobeedoo?

Fat Cat's eyes narrowed. Her fur stood up.
But Thelonious *had* to finish the song. He simply *had* to.

Thelonious waved his tail back and forth, very slowly, right under Fat Cat's nose. He sang, in a hypnotizing voice, as deep as a mouse could go,

"You need to keep the beat . . . I am no kitty treat . . . No, no, I'm way too hot to eat!

I am Thelonious, harmonious, and you are all alonious, I see,

so help me keep the beat, SO HELP ME! Move those furry, purry feet!"

Fat Cat heaved. Fat Cat sighed. Fat Cat followed that tail back and forth, back and forth, wide-eyed.

Then she let out a hum, a low-down, far from humdrum hum.

Her hips twitched. She slapped one paw on the floor. She tappity-tap-tapped with the other. Her tail swung to the beat. Then she sprang to her feet!

Fat Cat howled in harmony and danced as Thelonious sang,

"No more boohooings, no deadly doings, yahoo, pretty kitty!

Who knew we two could hop to a cuckoo duet, dum-ditty?"

Now his sister and brothers whistle as they hunt for scraps to share with Thelonious. They love the way his musical, mousical pinging and singing keeps Glad Cat busy. Yes, that cat's now so cool the mice *had* to change her name. They simply *had* to.